Touchstone Pictu...

HIDALGO

The Junior Novelization

TOUCHSTONE PICTURES PRESENTS A CASEY SILVER PRODUCTION A JOE JOHNSTON FILM VIGGO MORTENSEN "HIDALGO" OMAR SHARIF SAID TAGHMAOUI
MUSIC BY JAMES NEWTON HOWARD SPECIAL VISUAL EFFECTS AND ANIMATION BY INDUSTRIAL LIGHT & MAGIC COSTUME DESIGNER JEFFREY KURLAND
FILM EDITOR ROBERT DALVA PRODUCTION DESIGNER BARRY ROBISON DIRECTOR OF PHOTOGRAPHY SHELLY JOHNSON, ASC EXECUTIVE PRODUCER DON ZEPFEL PRODUCED BY CASEY SILVER
WRITTEN BY JOHN FUSCO DIRECTED BY JOE JOHNSTON hidalgo.movies.com Touchstone Pictures

ISBN: 0-7364-2169-6
Library of Congress Control Number: 2002116480
Printed in the United States of America
10 9 8 7 6 5 4 3 2

Touchstone Pictures

HIDALGO

The Junior Novelization

Adapted by Kim Ostrow

Based on the screenplay
by John Fusco
Produced by Casey Silver
Directed by Joe Johnston
Still photography by
Richard J. Cartwright

Random House 🏠 New York

Chapter 1

It was 1890 in the American West.

The sun rose over the Cheyenne River country. The land was peaceful and still. Suddenly, a vision appeared in the high grass. It was a stallion—moving with the natural grace of a dawn breeze. The horse ran free, hauntingly silhouetted against the flaming orange-red of the sun. His mane was long and wild. He was magnificent. A sight to see. A small, tough beast with patches of different colors and a flowing Spanish mane—his name was Hidalgo.

In the distance, a man whistled. Hidalgo threw his head high, ears alert. He began at an easy trot down to the other side of the bluff.

He stopped at a dead campfire site where a cowboy was packing his gear. The man was young in years, but his face was weathered. He was a cowboy through and through and a former Pony Express rider—some even said the last of his breed.

"Checkout time," said Frank Hopkins, squinting and gauging the position of the rising sun.

Hidalgo snorted, eager to get a move on. Frank flipped his saddle blanket over the pinto's back, adjusting it at the withers, and then swung the saddle up and onto the horse.

At another dying campfire sat a handsome man in a vest and jodhpurs. He was a well-known New England equestrian named Preston Webb.

"They're all well behind us, Senator," Webb said to his horse as he shaved. "When we cross the finish line, the box cameras will be flashing powder like it's Chinese New Year. We had best look like champions."

Webb finished up his shave and looked to

his big bay Thoroughbred. Then he checked the vast grasslands behind him. No one was in sight. Webb breathed in the cool morning air and pulled on his leather gloves. It was time to continue.

Later, when saddled up and on the move, Webb and his horse leaped over the ruins of an old buck-rail fence. Webb whipped his horse with a fancy leather crop. His horse was frothing, overheated and tired. They both were—but Webb could taste the victory.

Just then, Frank Hopkins and Hidalgo moved like pure speed over the grass. They passed over the same rail fence with the kind of grace that only comes from a horse and rider who share one mind, one heart. Together they galloped into badlands and canyon country with a purpose. They wanted to win.

Webb immediately looked over his shoulder when he heard the thunderous galloping behind him. It didn't take long for Frank to catch up to Webb.

"You went off the wagon trail," Webb said. "You went overland."

"Cross-country race, ain't it?" asked Frank.

Webb sat up tall. "I did not come twelve hundred miles to finish in second place!"

Frank smiled slyly. "Then why did ya?"

Webb took his crop and whipped his tired horse savagely. The Thoroughbred lurched ahead.

"The race is mine!" Webb shouted, a wicked grin spreading across his face as he left Frank and Hidalgo in the dust. Frank watched the poor fool as he cleared forty, fifty, sixty yards! The city slicker glanced over his shoulder to make sure he was still in the lead.

Frank leaned in close to Hidalgo's mane and whispered in the horse's ear, "I'm ready if you are."

And with that, he pushed his hat down tightly on his head and hunched in the saddle with his knees gripping the rough leather. "Let 'er buck!" he shouted.

Hidalgo took off like a painted cannonball! His legs blurred; his mane and tail flew in the wind. In only a matter of seconds, Frank and Hidalgo breezed past Webb and his mount.

With all he had, Webb flailed his horse's lathered hide, but the poor horse had nothing left. All Webb could do was watch as Frank and Hidalgo pulled farther and farther away from him. The outskirts of town were now visible on the horizon.

Frank and Hidalgo trotted effortlessly over the finish line. The people of Rapid City, South Dakota, cheered as Frank and Hidalgo waltzed through town.

The flashes of the camera powder had already faded by the time Preston Webb and Senator crossed the line . . . in second place.

Later, Webb walked into the hotel saloon. He looked around the crowded room, but no one looked back—they were all too busy congratulating Frank Hopkins. Race fans listened to his stories while the dance-hall beauties pined for the rough-and-ready cowboy. Webb's face turned red with anger. He stomped over to Frank.

"I don't like your style, Hopkins," Webb said gruffly.

The crowd went silent.

"And I don't like your horse," he added.

"He's said some real nice things about you," Frank said with a mischievous grin.

A few men chuckled, but there was tension in the air.

Webb took a step closer. "Mustangs don't belong in the same race as Thoroughbreds. If you ask me, they belong in fertilizer."

Frank stared at Webb. He finished his drink in one quick gulp. "You can say anything you want about me, mister. But don't go saying that about my horse."

Webb took the bait and raised his fists. Frank pulled a coin from the winnings in his leather bag. "Call it," Frank said, throwing the coin in the air. Slightly confused, Webb looked up at the flying coin. And then—*Pow!*—Frank punched him square on the chin and knocked Webb right off his feet. Frank caught the coin before Webb hit the ground. "Tails," said Frank, dropping the coin at Webb's feet. He hefted his bag of earnings over his shoulder and headed to the hotel lobby.

Frank stopped at the counter to get his room key.

"Somebody's waitin' for you, Hopkins," said the hotel clerk, handing him his key.

"Mr. Hopkins? Private Abernathy with the Fifth," said a young man in uniform, approaching the cowboy.

"Miles send you all the way from Fort Lincoln to congratulate me?" Frank asked.

The private appeared nervous but answered succinctly, "No sir."

"Didn't think so," said Frank.

The private handed Frank a leather dispatch case embossed with a U.S. stamp.

"Major Whiteside, Second Battalion, Seventh Cavalry Encampment at Wounded Knee Creek," the soldier said to clarify the situation.

Frank accepted his mission with a tired half salute. The fun was over. He had an important message to deliver.

At Wounded Knee Creek, thirty-five Minniconjou Sioux danced in a sunwise circle.

Most of the Indians wore Ghost Dance shirts, but some just wore blankets. As they sang, puffs of their breath appeared in the cold air.

As the sun rose, the dawn light fell upon two camps pitched near the creek. In one camp were four hundred Seventh Cavalry soldiers and enlisted men. Big cavalry horses were hitched to posts outside. There were army supplies littered all over the frozen ground. Four massive Hotchkiss mountain guns were pointed toward the wide creek below, where another camp was set up. Inside the second camp were three hundred and fifty Minniconjou and Hunkpapa Indians—men, women, and children living in dirty tents. The Ghost Dance was being performed to welcome the sun—but mostly to keep the half-frozen and hungry men and women warm.

Chief Big Foot, the leader of the tribe, was dying of pneumonia. He sat outside his tent, wrapped in a government blanket, repairing an old rifle. The old man looked up when he heard one of the soldiers shout, "Courier!" His tired eyes witnessed Frank Hopkins on his beautiful horse as he handed off the dispatch case to a young soldier.

Inside the officers' quarters, Major Whiteside took the leather case that Frank had delivered. The major was a grizzled old military man with a white beard. He huddled over the glowing potbellied stove, army blanket around his shoulders, as he began to read the official parchment.

"Disarm the Indians. Take every precaution to prevent their escape." Major Whiteside put down the letter and warmed his hands over the fire. Then he alerted the captain.

Meanwhile, Frank was tightening Hidalgo's cinch down in the creek bed. He couldn't help noticing the soldiers. They seemed nervous or frightened about something. Just then, a group of women from the Ghost Dance circle start to trill. This otherworldly singing startled a young corporal who was dipping buckets from the creek.

"They've been doing it all night. Gonna be an uprising," the corporal said, approaching Frank.

"No, soldier. Ghost Dance. That's all," Frank corrected him. The soldier looked up at Frank, confused.

"Praying to their ancestors for help," Frank said stoically, looking into the distance. "It's all they have left."

Just then, an old squaw holding an infant began to make her way toward Frank and the soldier.

"She know you, courier?" asked the soldier. Frank shook his head.

"Give her a swig of brandy. She'll go away," said the soldier before heading back to the creek and leaving Frank alone with the old woman.

"Chief Big Foot is dying in his lungs," she said to Frank in Lakota. "He spoke of you. Tell me. Where are they taking us?"

Frank surprised her by answering in her native language. "Tell the chief that the Long Knives are taking him to Pine Ridge. To hold council with Chief Red Cloud. He must do as they say."

One of the soldiers walked over to them, and Frank looked away so he would not see the soldier push the old woman to the ground.

"Get behind the tent line!" the soldier shouted.

The old woman pulled herself to her feet, still cradling the infant. She held out a hand to Frank and told him she knew his mother. But the soldier interrupted by pushing her in the direction of the clustered teepees.

Frank whistled to Hidalgo, and then mounted his horse. The mustang broke into a defiant trot through the frosty weeds, away from Wounded Knee and far away from something Frank wanted no part of.

At the edge of the Lakota prison camp, soldiers moved into the ravine. They cruelly pulled rifles from the hands of old men. They savagely stormed the tents and brought out axes, knives, crowbars—anything that might be used as a weapon. A young deaf Indian fought the soldiers who were trying to take his hunting rifle. He did not understand what was happening. The fighting and the confusion grew more frenzied. The soldiers began to lose control of the situation.

But Frank Hopkins was long gone. And he never looked back. Hidalgo and Frank trotted down the military road. It was cold, and snow began to sprinkle the trail.

Suddenly, Hidalgo slowed. Frank tried to adjust his speed, but Hidalgo jogged off the trail, turned around, and tossed his mane.

"What you doing, bronco?" Frank asked. "Keep on, now."

Hidalgo's eyes stared out across the Great Plains with the wary look of an intelligent animal that could sense danger. Frank assumed Hidalgo was reacting to an approaching tornado or perhaps a coyote in the distance. But in an instant, a terrible sound was carried over the horizon. This thunder did not belong to a rain cloud. It was the distant sound of machine-gun fire.

Hidalgo was rapidly snorting the frosty air. Frank turned him around to face where they had come from. The gunfire kept on and on. Frank dug his heels into Hidalgo's sides, and the mustang headed back toward the cavalry camp.

When they got to Wounded Knee Creek, Frank slowed Hidalgo to a trot as they came to the top of a bluff. From there, they could see what was happening.

Soldiers stood on the ridges overlooking the frozen riverbed. Most of them looked shell-shocked; some were being sick. Frank stopped Hidalgo. It was then that he saw. Three hundred Lakota Indians gunned down. All were dead in the ravine.

Frank looked like a man impaled through the chest—as if all this had happened directly to him. Soldiers moved around him, but all he could hear was the sound of his own heart beating in his ears.

Chapter 2

Eighteen months later, a drunken, unwashed, and unshaven Frank Hopkins sat backstage at *Buffalo Bill's Wild West Show: The Romantic West Brought East in Reality*. William Cody, also known as Buffalo Bill, was the entrepreneur responsible for staging reenactments of the Battle of Wounded Knee under a circus tent. Frank and Hidalgo rode around the tent while the crowds cheered. But the shows were awful, and Frank was miserable. He wore a spotless white ten-gallon hat—he was playing the good guy. Frank felt anything but good.

"Mothers, hold on to your children!" shouted Buffalo Bill through a megaphone.

"This is not an act. You are beholding the last of the wild hostiles."

A majestic older Indian in full warrior attire stood by Frank backstage.

"What says Long Hair about me?" Chief Eagle Horn asked Frank, in Lakota.

"He said here comes a great and honorable man," Frank said.

Chief Eagle Horn stared at Frank. "Far Rider. You are not a good liar."

The chief smiled at Frank. He still had a sense of humor—even in this ridiculous carnival he had to perform in. Frank smiled back.

Later that day, the whole show piled into a twenty-seven-car steam train. As it chugged through the rain, Hidalgo rested his head against the slatted boards of the car he rode in. He looked out over the passing landscape.

In the bar car sat Buffalo Bill Cody and Nate Salisbury, the show manager.

"We can count and recount the gate receipts all night, Bill. The fact is, if you keep hiring on every Calamity Jane or Indian Joe you ever knew, we'll be lucky to break even."

"I hire those who were the West. You don't like it, stay in New York," said Buffalo Bill. "Now let me see what we did in Kansas."

Frank was playing cards at a nearby table. Just then, Chief Eagle Horn walked slowly down the aisle, stopping when he reached Frank. He spoke in Lakota.

"Far Rider. I must speak to Long Hair. Please, speak United States for me."

Frank accompanied the chief, who spoke slow and eloquent Lakota.

"He says he respects you for your kindness," Frank translated for Buffalo Bill. Nate Salisbury looked up impatiently.

"I see. Tell the chief that the respect is mutual. Also, tell him I have fresh oyster stew for him in the kitchen car."

Buffalo Bill looked over to Salisbury. "Look at this man, Nate. You want me to replace him with a painted street bum?"

Frank continued. "The chief says his people

are vanishing faster than he can earn silver."

Buffalo Bill's eyes softened. "This is how we keep his people alive. Through instructive presentation."

Salisbury was getting annoyed. He had no time for this.

Frank explained that the chief's nation was broken and scattered, their buffalo had been destroyed, and the government had herded their wild horses into corrals. He said there was word those horses would be destroyed, too.

"Tell my dear friend Eagle Horn that the mustang breed has known its day and served its purpose. If my chief wishes a fine horse, I will give him a Thoroughbred steed of his chosen color. Tell him," said Buffalo Bill.

Frank didn't want to waste the chief's time with such nonsense. Instead, he passed on Eagle Horn's final statement.

"The government has put a price on the native horses. A price too great for poor people to meet. He says that perhaps his people have lost their lands, but not their spirit. He asks you, his friend and a great man, for your help."

Buffalo Bill looked out the window and sipped his drink. "Tell my American brother that I miss those wild days as much as he does. And that I have nothing but respect for his proud history. I will do all that I can to honor the interest of my red brethren."

Franks stared hard into Buffalo Bill's eyes as he finished his drink. Frank recognized something familiar there. It was the dull look of shame.

Days later, the Wild West show was up in Coney Island, New York—and it was a big hit. The Eastern crowd hollered with glee and watched in awe as Buffalo Bill roped six Indians at one time.

In a box seat sat a young Arab man with a cool-eyed blond man named Rasmussen. "What do you think of the show, Aziz?" the blond man asked.

Aziz looked at him without uttering a word.

Offstage, Buffalo Bill shouted through his megaphone.

"Over three hundred endurance-ride victories, folks. Here they are. You remember them. The world's greatest long-distance race team, rough-riding Frank Hopkins and his horse, Hidalgo!"

Unfortunately, Frank had been drinking and was having a difficult time staying on his horse. Frank tried to hold on as Hidalgo gained speed and circled the tent. The crowd cheered! Hidalgo made a cutting turn and Frank began to fall . . . but the horse was quick enough to cut back and keep Frank in the saddle. Just then, Hidalgo broke into a gallop. He charged the stand and came to a sudden stop. Frank went flying into the audience! The crowd groaned at the cowboy's bad luck as he lay there, sprawled out and staring at the circus top.

Thinking fast, one of the actresses backstage yelled to Buffalo Bill, "The wounded soldier trick!"

"Ladies and gentleman," shouted Buffalo Bill. "Let's hear it for the wounded soldier trick!"

The crowd burst into applause. Frank lay

still, stunned. Hidalgo ran over to Frank, sniffed at him a little, then picked up Frank's hat in his big teeth and handed it to him. The crowd roared with laughter. Then Hidalgo took a mouthful of Frank's shirt and began to back away slowly and steadily, dragging Frank across the ground.

"And the horse drags the wounded soldier home!" shouted Buffalo Bill into his megaphone.

The crowd hooted and hollered once again as Hidalgo dragged his cowboy through the dirt. What the crowd didn't know was that none of this was in the script.

At intermission, Buffalo Bill sat at his desk, smoking a thin cigar and counting gate receipts. His long wig was sitting on the desk, exposing his shiny bald head. But when Salisbury cleared his throat to announce that Bill had a visitor, the old cowboy quickly placed his fake locks back on his head.

"These gentlemen would like to see you. They're from the Middle East. Businessmen," said Salisbury.

"A great honor, Mr. Cody. My name is Rau

Rasmussen," said one of the men. "I present to you Mr. Bin Aziz, a representative of Sheikh bin Riyadh of Qunfidha."

Buffalo Bill Cody smiled at the two men. "Welcome indeed. I hope you aren't leaving before Act Three and Custer's Last Stand."

"We are most interested in this rough-riding Frank Hopkins and his horse," said Rasmussen.

"He was rough tonight, wasn't he? Nate! Get Hopkins in here," ordered Buffalo Bill. "What is your business, Mr. Rasmussen?"

"Shipping, sir. I control the transport trade between Aden and Gaza. The great sheikh is a business partner," he said.

"And he wishes to invest in the Cody enterprise?" asked Buffalo Bill.

"The sheikh of sheikhs, His Greatness, is beyond investment. His pride is in his family horses," said Aziz.

Buffalo Bill looked at Aziz quizzically. "And you are who, again?" he asked.

Rasmussen continued. "You see, Mr. Cody,

Sheikh Riyadh is keeper of the Muniqiyah stallion."

Buffalo Bill didn't understand what these two strangers were talking about.

"His Excellency's royal stables preserve the purest equine bloodline in the world," Rasmussen explained.

"Legend claims that the Muniqiyah descend from the original five strains of the Prophet's followers," added Aziz.

Rasmussen tried to make it clear to Buffalo Bill. "The sheikh's own stallion, al-Hattal, is the greatest living endurance-race champion of all time."

"I am already intrigued by this Arabian horse," said Buffalo Bill. "Does this sultan wish to display him in my show?"

"Sheik bin Riyadh himself saw your show in Paris. His Honor was deeply insulted by your claim to exhibit the world's greatest endurance horse and rider," said Rasmussen.

Buffalo Bill smirked at his guests. "Hidalgo

is a legend, my friends. He has never lost a long-distance race. Never."

"In America, perhaps," said Aziz. "On deserts that a woman from my country could cross on foot."

Just then, Salisbury entered the office with Frank. He looked a mess and was still dusty from his fall.

Buffalo Bill put his arm around Frank. "You just missed some wonderful compliments about your horse. Gentlemen, I present rough-riding Frank Hopkins."

"Mr. Hopkins. A pleasure," said Rasmussen.

Frank tipped his hat, then looked around the tent.

Aziz got down to business. "Mr. Cody. His Excellency, the Great Sheikh of Qunfidha, requests you remove the title you have bestowed on this American horse."

"What's going on here, Bill?" grumbled Frank.

"Gentlemen, I welcome your excellent

sheikh to my show anytime, anywhere, as my guest," said Buffalo Bill. "But no one . . . no one tells me how to promote or advertise my Wild West."

Aziz and Rasmussen discreetly exchanged a hard look.

"It is understood, sir," said Aziz, staring at Frank's dusty boots. Frank was staring at Aziz's scimitar.

"Perhaps you have never heard of the Ocean of Fire," said Rasmussen. "The great horse race of the bedouin. It has been held annually for more than one thousand years. A three-thousand-mile race. Across the Arabian desert, along the Persian Gulf and Iraq, and across the sands of Syria to Damascus."

"Hell, that ain't a race. That's an expedition," said Frank.

Aziz spoke plainly. "Our office will accept your entry at one thousand dollars in Spanish silver."

Frank looked at Buffalo Bill. The old

cowboy met his gaze—both realized that the stakes had just gotten higher. The two visitors waited.

"The winner's purse, sir, makes the victor very honored . . . very, how do you say . . . ," Aziz began.

"Very rich, Mr. Cody," Rasmussen translated.

"Three thousand miles," Frank pondered out loud, rubbing his rough, dirty chin.

"It is not a game," assured Aziz. "Who survives, wins."

Frank shook his head. "These boys are serious, Bill."

"His Greatness invites you and your horse to enter the great challenge—if you will not remove the title that you have bestowed upon the impure animal," Aziz said.

"Impure? He's pure mustang, friend," Frank guaranteed.

"Then prove your claim to the title. In the Ocean of Fire," Aziz challenged the cowboy.

Frank stuffed his hands in his pockets. "I don't race no more, mister."

"What shall I tell His Excellency?" asked Aziz impatiently.

"Tell him to go pound sand for all I care," Frank grumbled.

Aziz pulled out his sword. "Blasphemy!"

Buffalo Bill—just as fast as his opponent—drew his Colt .44 and pointed it at Aziz.

"Put it away, my Arabian friend," Buffalo Bill warned.

"Mr. Cody, please. Amend your unholy claims. Or you will hear from the great family of bin Riyadh again," promised Aziz.

Aziz sheathed his scimitar and Cody holstered his gun.

"The third act is starting, gentlemen. I suggest you take your seats," said Buffalo Bill.

With that, Aziz and Rasmussen got up to leave. At the tent entrance, Aziz stopped and turned around. "A wise choice you have made, Mr. Hopkins," he said with a cold, charming smile. He stared Frank in the eye for a moment, and then, as if satisfied with what he saw there, Aziz quietly turned and exited the tent.

Later that day, Frank stumbled into his dressing room. A single slash of daylight cut through the darkness. His shirt was untucked and unbuttoned as he headed toward his small desk to pay a visit to a bottle of tequila. As he uncorked the bottle, he caught a glimpse of himself in a small stage mirror. He stared hard, barely recognizing the man staring back. He took off his ten-gallon hat and searched his eyes for whoever was left in there.

Outside his tent, Frank could hear the shrill sounds of Buffalo Bill's megaphone and gunshots echoing across the arena. The phoniness of show life was getting under his skin. With the bottle in his hand, he edged the mirror off his desk. It fell to the straw-covered ground. Just then, he felt eyes upon him.

"Long Hair has promised me rock candy in

Pittsburgh. When do we reach Pittsburgh, Far Rider?" asked Chief Eagle Horn, stepping from the shadows outside the tent.

"Two days, maybe three," said Frank.

The chief entered Frank's tent and sat in front of him. Studying Frank for a moment, the old man could see the torment in his eyes.

"Will you and your pony be going to Pittsburgh?" asked the chief.

Frank didn't respond. He picked up his old hat and worked the crease back into it. He looked for an answer in his heart, but he didn't have one.

"They say our good red and blue days are over. Perhaps all of us will die in this show of the great Cody," said Chief Eagle Horn. "You have a chance to go save yourself, Far Rider."

"Hidalgo is not the horse he used to be," admitted Frank.

"Is it better to perish here . . . in this Wild West as Cody tells it?" the chief asked.

Frank was quiet for a moment, thinking deeply about what the chief had asked. "I saw what happened at Wounded Knee Creek,"

Frank said. "I carried the orders from the army."

Chief Eagle Horn stared into the distance. "You did not know."

The two men sat in silence. Then the chief spoke again. "I call you Far Rider not because of your great races or your fine pony, but because you are one who rides far from himself. And wishes not to look home. Until you do . . . you are neither white man nor Indian. You are lost."

Frank looked into the face of the great Indian chief who sat before him, and slowly made up his mind.

When the steam whistle blew and the steel wheels ground against the rail, the cattle door of the train rolled open, and Frank and Hidalgo leaped from the moving train. Anyone watching would have seen a painted mustang hitting the dirt and flying down the track, toward the city buildings.

It was time for Frank and Hidalgo to race again.

Chapter 3

Frank rode Hidalgo all the way back to the docks in New York Harbor. When he spotted Rasmussen, he galloped over and dropped a bag of money at his feet.

"The house of Sheikh bin Riyadh will be greatly honored," said Rasmussen, smiling. Frank nodded and rode Hidalgo straight up the freight gangplank of the *City of Paris*—the ocean liner that would take them far across the sea.

Once safely aboard, Frank stood at the rail, watching the majestic Statue of Liberty as he sailed by. What he didn't see was Aziz watching him from the upper promenade. The man was surprised that Frank had accepted the challenge. What a race it would be.

Meanwhile, Hidalgo was furiously pacing in his stall. Next to him was a chestnut Arabian mare draped in velvet blankets. She traveled well, but Hidalgo was feeling boxed in and his wild side was coming out.

A group of merchant sailors, amused by Hidalgo's behavior, began poking him with the handle of a shovel. In defense, Hidalgo stomped his front hooves. One sailor laughed and turned to his friends. But all he saw was a punch coming straight at him. He dropped straight to the ground. The five other merchant sailors grabbed for Frank, trying to keep him away from their chief. But Frank spun on his heels and elbowed one of the sailors in the chest. Then he hit another one. After that, he wrestled two more to the ground.

Meanwhile, the first sailor had gotten up and grabbed a boiler room wrench. *Crack!* He hit Frank over the head. As Frank went down, he fell square into another sailor's knee. Hidalgo was going insane, trying to burst out and help Frank. The sailor was setting up to really let Frank have it with the huge wrench when he heard the double click of a gun. It was Aziz—with a revolver aimed directly at the sailor's head.

Painfully, Frank rolled over. He looked up in a daze and saw a well-dressed woman standing behind Aziz's shoulder.

"Are you all right, sir?" she asked.

Frank tried to lift himself to answer the handsome woman but fell instead. A trickle of blood ran down his weathered face as he lost consciousness.

Later that night, Frank was recovering in the first-class lounge in the company of Major and Lady Anne Davenport of England. Frank held an ice bag to his head as the major looked on, delighted to examine a real live cowboy up close.

"Ice is a precious commodity in Arabia, my friend. My gin might go warm for the sake of your misfortune," Major Davenport said good-naturedly.

"Obliged. But I'll take a warm gin over ice any day, mister," Frank answered, taking the tumbler the man offered him.

"Major. Major Davenport," the man corrected. "And my wife, Lady Anne Davenport of Byron. They tell me you put on quite a Wild West display down there in steerage."

"Rasmussen's merchants are an ugly lot. You handled them with aplomb. Well done," said Lady Anne, taking a seat near Frank. She admired the cowboy at close range. "Is it true, then, Mr. Hopkins, that you are en route to Aden to enter your horse in the famous race?"

"Can't think of another reason to cross the ocean, ma'am," Frank said.

"He is the real item, isn't he?" the major asked his wife jovially. "The vernacular is lovely. Mr. Hopkins, please humor me. Have you ever killed any red Indians?"

Frank looked at the major, digesting the ugly but often-asked question. He drank down the glass of gin before answering. "Just one. A long time ago . . ."

Lady Anne stared at the handsome rough rider. "Do you know whom you are racing against?" she asked.

"A hundred Arabians is the word," Frank said matter-of-factly.

"Not just one hundred Arabians, Mr. Hopkins. One hundred of the finest and purest horses ever bred."

Lady Anne listed all the famous horses he would be competing against, leaving for last Shakra, the white racer descended from the great al-Jabella.

"And who owns that one?" Frank mused. "The Queen of Sheba?"

"No, Mr. Hopkins. I do," Lady Anne said, meeting Frank's smiling eyes with her own. Frank looked away first, slightly embarrassed.

"Lady Davenport has lived among the bedouins. She speaks fluent Arabic and Kurdistani. And what is the African dialect you study, love?" the major asked his wife.

But Lady Anne had other questions on her mind. "What breed is your stud, Mr. Hopkins?"

"Hidalgo is a mustang," Frank said boldly.

Major Davenport, never having heard such a word, looked puzzled.

"From the Spanish *mesteño*. Means untamed. It is the horse of the red Indian. Small. Hearty. Mixed blood of Spanish origin," said Lady Davenport.

"Well, my young American friend, you will not be racing red Indians. And you will not be crossing the purple sage of the Wild West. You will be racing bedouin nomads and athletes born to the sands. Across a desert, where if the sun won't drive you mad by day, the cold will freeze your blood by night," warned the major.

"Thank you for the encouragement, Major. And for the gin," Frank said, getting up to leave. He tipped his hat to Lady Anne. She bade him good night and stared intently as the cowboy sauntered out of their room.

"I find him rather charming. Do you?" asked the major. Lady Anne did not seem to have heard the question, but a distant smile crossed her face as she watched the cowboy leave.

Chapter
4

Days later, the *City of Paris* pulled into the port of Aden, Saudi Arabia. It was a scorching hot day in the exotic land. Camel bells and steam horns echoed across the sea; men in head cloths speaking Arabic milled about; and women with veils covering their faces watched the boat arrivals from the shade of the market tents.

Frank, clean-shaven and handsome, came down the ship's gangway, leading Hidalgo. Frank looked around to take in the foreign land before him. A clutch of British soldiers with rifles and brass cartridge belts passed by merchants speaking in Arabic, Turkish, and French. Hidalgo's ears stood up high as if he were spooked as a large, long-necked camel crossed his path. And another. Then a small herd of camels passed by, plodding across the dock. Crowds of children surrounded the painted horse and the cowboy in hat and boots. They touched Frank's holster, his rope, and his saddle.

"Most have never seen an American," Aziz explained. "Please follow me to the caravan."

Frank, on Hidalgo, followed Aziz along the camel route to the tent city. He watched Lady Anne, ahead of him in the procession, scold her attendants in fluent Arabic. Her sharp words sent them to cool her horse's leg with wet towels. Frank also saw twenty slaves being herded along on foot, looking thirsty and miserable.

"And you thought your west was wild," Aziz said, seeing Frank's reaction. "Welcome to Arabia."

In the tent city of Aden, some three hundred tents of all shapes and colors were spread over the white sand. Arabian music played all around. The wild gestures and buzzing activity among the various groups of men told Frank that high-stakes bets were being made.

Suddenly, Frank saw something appear, lit by the flamelike glow of the sunset—it was the silhouette of the most incredible horse he'd ever seen. A classic Arabian, rearing and slashing his hooves at the sky. On his back was a young and handsome prince, wearing a head cloth and a robe with long lappets hanging from the sleeves. There was a gold scimitar snug on his belt. This was Bin al-Reeh. The prince controlled the horse with perfect confidence.

With a great arched neck and high tail, al-Hattal stood sixteen hands tall. The horse's muscles jumped under the tight sheen of jet-black skin. He didn't whinny like most horses—he wailed like a banshee. Nine handlers moved alongside the stallion and the great prince. This was a sight to see, and Frank couldn't take his eyes off it.

"Equine perfection," said an equally awed Lady Anne.

At the center of the camp stood the sheikh's great tent. Six armed men and one massive black bodyguard protected it. At the entrance stood a woman in a crimson silk robe with silver bracelets encircling her arms. A soft muslin veil masked her face so that only her striking eyes were visible. She entered the shade of the luxurious tent to talk with her father, the sheikh.

"He is a fine young man of royal pedigree. Educated in the mission school, well read. He owns sixty-four villages and vast cultivated lands." The sheikh spoke of the prince—the man he wanted his daughter to marry. But his speech was interrupted by his beautiful daughter, Jazira. She had let her veil drop. Her skin was a beautiful dark golden hue. "Father," she said.

"I pray only for your happiness," he responded.

"Be careful then, Father," she said. "Because I am happiest on a horse, riding where females are forbidden."

"There is a tempest in my tent. But it has come in the form of my cherished daughter to upset my pancreas," he replied with the weariness and pride of a father.

Just then they heard the caravan approaching. The sheikh called for his slave, Jaffa.

"The eastern caravan. It has arrived," said Jaffa.

"The good Lady Davenport?" asked the sheikh.

"Yes. And an American. On a horse of most unusual color," said Jaffa.

"The cowboy," the sheikh said under his breath.

Outside his own tent, Frank hitched Hidalgo to a post. He removed his hat and poured water from his canteen over his face and hair.

"How do you like it so far?" Frank asked his horse, taking in the exotic pulses of the music and language that surrounded them. Hidalgo took Frank's hat off the post and shoved it at him, hinting that he wanted to go home.

"Too late," Frank said, taking the hat back and punching in a crease.

"Very wise to tie your horse," Aziz said, walking up to Frank's tent. "If he was to cover an Arab mare, it would be viewed as a most inviolable blemish. The foal would need to be destroyed before it touched the ground. As would the offending sire."

Frank leaned into Hidalgo and gave him a brotherly poke in the side. "You hear that? Keep your pride tucked."

"You are summoned as a guest of His Excellency, Sheikh bin Riyadh," Aziz said.

Jaffa, the giant bodyguard, stood behind Aziz. He gestured for Frank to follow.

The sheikh was sitting on a woven mat atop a large number of Oriental rugs and cushions on the sand floor of his lodgings.

"In the name of Allah, I welcome you into my tent as my guest," said the sheikh. Frank offered his hand to shake, but the sheikh did not accept.

"If His Excellency were to touch an infidel,

he would lose his ability to foretell the future," Aziz explained.

The sheikh showed Frank to a rug and then ordered Aziz to leave them to talk. Jaffa knelt to pour the sheikh some coffee, but he motioned for it to be served first to Frank.

"Most *farengi* find our coffee to be too potent," he said.

But Frank downed it without hesitation. "Back home, we toss a horseshoe into the pot. If it stands straight up, coffee's ready."

The sheikh was silent. Frank toasted him with the small, delicate cup of coffee.

"Revive thy spirit, then! Shall we play at cards? Perhaps cribbage?"

"I'm not much of a gambler," Frank said.

"To the contrary. You are gambling with your very life in the great race," said the sheikh.

"Life I can handle. Money gets away from me," Frank joked.

The sheikh wasn't smiling. "Life can get away from us at times also, Mr. Hopkins. The desert is the great leveler."

Just then, Frank felt eyes on him. He turned to find Jazira staring at him from the shadows. Only her eyes were visible above her veil. Frank removed his hat, but Jazira drew back uneasily.

"I had five sons once. Three killed in the raids. One perished in this very race six years ago. The other swallowed by the quicksand of the Hammad. I am now a man with no sons. Just one lowly daughter. Please, for my honor and yours, ignore her presence."

Frank slowly looked away from Jazira as she vanished into the night. The sheikh continued.

"I am greatly pleased that you have accepted my challenge. But I must warn you: never before has a foreigner partaken in the great race. Some are angry. They find the entry of a mongrel horse an insult to this sport of sultans."

"I'm not here to insult anybody, sir," Frank said. "I'm just here to race. And then go home."

The sheikh stared at Frank. He was fascinated by the cowboy's spurs, the pearl-handled Colt in his holster, and his intensity.

"You have two days to prepare your charger

for the starting gun. You are under my protection. Even as I defeat you and win your money," said the sheikh, eyeing the cowboy before him, looking for a sign of weakness. "What is the most you have ever won in a horse race?"

"Three thousand," answered Frank.

"That is much," said the sheikh, drawing on his smoking pipe. "The winner's purse in the Ocean of Fire exceeds one hundred thousand in American currency."

Frank nearly choked.

"But that matters very little to me," said the sheikh. "What matters to my house is honor. Our culture revolves around it. The purity of the blood in our horses is as uncompromised as our faith. Victory is not a game. My family's stable has never lost this race."

Suddenly, the sound of a horse startled Frank. Two handlers were leading al-Hattal right into the tent. The stallion was blanketed in silks and velvet. The handlers formally greeted their sheikh and then led the horse to a luxurious area in the big tent, where a white companion horse, a gelded Arabian, was hitched.

"On cold nights, my wives sleep in the stable tents so that al-Hattal is comfortable and appeased. Jaffa? Show Mr. Hopkins to his tent. He needs his rest."

Frank tipped his hat courteously to the sheikh as he headed out.

"Mr. Hopkins," said the sheikh, "I will amend the winner's purse with another ten thousand if you will put that Colt pistol in the pot. That is an authentic Colt, is it not?"

Frank smiled at his host. "Well, as they say back home, God didn't make all men equal. Mr. Colt did."

"God did not make all men equal, Mr. Hopkins. Nor any mortal. You will find this out. Will you wager this magnificent weapon?"

Frank nodded. "At the end of the race," he said.

"Very good," said the sheikh. "Sleep well, and blessed be thee."

In the tent city that night, there was almost absolute quiet. All lights were out, and the camels and horses were asleep. In true cowboy fashion, Frank slept under the stars, covered by an Indian wool blanket. His perfectly creased hat was tipped over his eyes. Yusuf, a slave the sheikh had instructed to assist Frank, snored in his tent like a camel with a bad cold.

From out of the darkness, a stranger crept into the camp on silent feet and approached Hidalgo. The horse snorted and flattened his ears. The stranger approached in a slow and careful manner, letting Hidalgo smell an outstretched hand. At the slightest of sounds, Frank flipped his brim back and took out his Colt sidearm. He turned around to face the intruder.

Hidalgo was gone!

Frank rolled to his feet. He broke into a run over the sand. As he came across the dunes with a rope and his gun ready to go, he whistled. Hidalgo broke free of the stranger and ran to his master. The stranger fled in the opposite direction. Frank hurled his rope with expert speed, catching the stranger's ankle. He whipped the intruder off the ground, and the stranger landed facefirst in the sand. Frank jumped from a dune, landing on the stranger, and stuck the barrel of his Colt up under the linen-wrapped chin.

The stranger's eyes focused intently on Frank under the bright light of the moon. Frank angrily yanked down the horse thief's linen muffler.

"Please! As my father has warned you, do not look upon me," said Jazira, cowering.

Frank was startled to see the lovely Jazira. She was more beautiful than he could ever have imagined. He stood as she pulled her muffler back up. "I mean no harm to your property."

"Then what were you doing stealing off with my horse?" Frank demanded.

"To examine what kind of sand hoof he has. To determine is he is capable of crossing the Rub al-Khali, the great desert."

Jazira was staring at Frank's gun. He holstered it.

"So the king can raise his bet?" he asked.

"Racing here is not like in your home," Jazira said. She produced some parchment from inside her robe and passed an ancient map to Frank. "I just wanted to see for myself if this animal has a chance of surviving. Because I fear that you do not."

"Beg your pardon, miss, but what stake do you have in me and my pony?" Frank asked. "We're the opposition."

Jazira was silent. She started to say something but stopped, as if changing her mind.

"A woman does not make her own choices, Mr. Frank."

"Still don't understand why you—"

"Please. It must not be known. I am my father's master of horses. I have a manner of speaking to the equines," she said.

"I know," said Frank. "My horse doesn't let strangers touch him."

Silence returned to the night sands. Jazira tried not to meet the cowboy's gaze.

"I can speak to the equines better than my brothers ever did. I see in your horse's eyes something rare. He has tremendous courage. But no horse stands a chance against al-Hattal. Attempt not to stay with Bin al-Reeh in the early weeks. Nor ride close to Lady Anne's Kurdistani boy—he will kill you with his scimitar."

Frank glanced at Jazira as she spoke. "Please, look away from me."

Frank did.

"At noon, hide from the sun beneath your robes, and do not fear the locusts; they are a gift from above, not a plague, as you might believe," Jazira said.

Just then, Frank saw a giant crossing over the dunes with his sword drawn.

"It's all right, Jaffa," called Jazira.

"Please. Your father will have my eyes if I lose sight of you, child," said Jaffa.

Jazira whispered to Jaffa in Arabic pleadingly, and the giant man retreated. Jazira began to slip away into he night.

"You saying you want your father's stallion to lose?" asked Frank.

"Mr. Frank, when you first looked upon me,

you removed your hat. Why?" she asked.

"You're a lady," Frank answered simply.

Jazira stared at the cowboy, thinking. Then Jaffa returned and whispered in her ear. She looked once more at Frank, and the two hurried silently across the sands toward the tents.

Frank calmed Hidalgo as he looked toward where the moon was fading and daylight edged closer. Then he looked back at the departing Jazira in the shadows. He was greatly confused by her, but he'd be a liar if he said he was not intrigued as well. Frank tucked the map into his back pocket and led Hidalgo back to camp.

A fiery sun burned brightly over the Arabian desert. Arabian horses were walked to the edge of the base camp. Excitement filled the air, thicker than desert dust. It was finally race day.

Frank watched all the horses begin to move toward the starting line. A big Arabian appeared. It was Lady Anne Davenport's mare. On the horse's back was a tall, handsome man from a Kurdish tribe. He wore the robes of royalty and carried the largest sword Frank had ever seen. The Kurd, as he was called, stared down at Frank with fierce eyes and a smile full of perfect white teeth. He rode to Lady Anne's side for inspection.

Another horseman passed by, this one with the face of a man who'd seen many hard summers in the desert. The rider carried a hooded falcon on his heavily gloved left wrist like a weapon.

"My name is Sakr, and desert law compels me to speak the truth," he said, circling Hidalgo. "I find the entry of a Westerner sacrilege. But I trust in Allah. And He will roast ten of us like sheep on a spit before the sun sets today. You shall be among the first. I say this."

"Don't count on it," Frank replied defiantly as Sakr rode down the line, showing off his horse's perfect gait.

The sight at the starting line was incredible. A regal formation of one hundred Arabian horses and bedouin riders, each twenty feet apart on the white sand. And, in the middle of it all, one of the last American cowboys on a mustang pony.

Prince Bin al-Reeh headed toward the starting line with an entourage of men. A slave got down on all fours, and the prince used his back as a stepstool to mount the seat of honor. Horses began to whinny and snort as they saw the horse that was coming—it was the great stallion al-Hattal, ridden by the young Bin al-Reeh. The magnificent horse and rider made their way past the competitors to take their place at the starting line.

The Saudi prince passed Frank and Hidalgo, circled them, and said something to his fellow riders in Arabic. The horsemen stared at Frank and then laughed.

"He says maybe we should give you a head start," translated Yusuf. But this talk didn't affect Frank. He just sat in his saddle, hat brim low, staring at the prince.

An old Arab man stood facing the starting line. He wore a robe with long lappets and wooden beads around his neck. He carefully examined the line from one end to the other, checking the position of the sun.

Two younger Arabs brought over an elaborate rosewood case. From it they removed an antique matchlock rifle and passed it to the ancient man in ceremonial robes. The man raised it to the sky and shouted in Arabic. Another old Arab man repeated his words in a louder, shriller voice for all to hear.

"Ride each day to sunset. Start again at dawn. Those who survive to reach the halfway camp on the Rub al-Khali shall be rewarded with a full day's rest before the final run. Strength to your horses, and may God have mercy on your souls."

Hundreds watched. Sakr removed the hood from his falcon, and the bird lofted high into the desert sun and headed north. Horses snorted. Riders fixed their eyes on the endless desert ahead.

And then—*boom!* The starting gun fired. The horses exploded off the starting line. Their journey across the great desert had begun. Hidalgo was right in the thick of it, as hot-blooded as any of the Arabian horses—but only for the first hundred yards. Then Frank and Hidalgo were left in the white dust.

"We'll never catch them. Not in the quarter-mile. We'll do it like we always do. They run pretty. But we last. Deal?" he said to his horse.

Bin al-Reeh looked down the line to see Frank's position. When he spotted them a quarter mile behind, he smiled and pointed them out to his fellow riders. Lady Anne's horse was keeping the prince's pace. Sakr also moved along swiftly. But Hidalgo was way behind.

Chapter
5

At high noon, Hidalgo's muscles were visible under his sweat-drenched coat. A strange wind blew up out of nowhere, moving the contours of the sand from small dunes into one massive ridge. Frank climbed over the great ridge. From there, he could see thirty horsemen loping toward the mountains. They looked as if they floated on the sand. The horses stayed fifty yards from each other. Suddenly, a handsome blue Arabian hit a split in the ground. The horse's legs buckled violently. The rider was pitched forward off the horse and rolled over in the sand. The other horsemen kept riding.

The rider crawled over to his horse and saw

that one of its legs was broken. He kissed the horse as the poor creature cried in pain. The rider looked toward the sky in prayer. Then he unsheathed his sword and swiftly ran it through his horse's chest. He embraced the Arabian's head and helped it to the ground gracefully. Then he began to walk away.

Frank watched all this from the top of the sand ridge. Unable to help himself, he signaled for Hidalgo to run to the Arabian's side.

Sakr noticed this and bolted to the cowboy's side. "No! Do not aid him! It is against the laws of the race!"

Frank watched as Sakr rode off into the distance to gain on the breakaway riders. But Frank could not leave the man stranded in the desert. The rider drew his sword and refused Frank's help.

"You'll die out here on foot, partner," pleaded Frank.

The rider turned from Frank. Then he impaled himself through his heart with his own sword!

Frank stared in disbelief. Hidalgo snorted at the smell of the man's blood. The cowboy took one last look at the rider, then pointed Hidalgo back toward the race. The wind blew sand over the body of the fallen man and his horse.

The race had only just begun.

At sunset, as the orange sun lowered over the horizon, Frank dismounted Hidalgo. He found a small oasis of scrub plants and frankincense trees near some of the other riders.

"Best hotel in town, I reckon," Frank said, setting Hidalgo free to feast upon the scrub plants. A small desert hare startled Hidalgo, but not Frank. He had use for the little creature. He quickly drew his Colt, but—*wham!* A falcon swooped in like a lightning bolt, snapping the hare's neck. Frank watched as Sakr dismounted his horse and retrieved the fresh kill, smiling at Frank's loss.

Later that night, Frank made coffee over a small campfire, watching his breath in the glow.

Hidalgo lay down next to him. Frank studied his parchment map until he was satisfied that he understood his route for the following day. Then he played a little harmonica for his and Hidalgo's entertainment.

"Cowboy!" Bin al-Reeh called from the darkness. "Nearly one hundred paces in one day. Most impressive."

"You boys are good," Frank admitted.

"This is your last chance to turn back. Hear me. You do not belong out here. Turn back at dawn, or prepare for a death beyond your greatest fear."

Frank did not answer the prince. His long silence spoke better than many words.

"Tomorrow I shall not even look over my shoulder," warned Bin al-Reeh.

"No need to, prince," said Frank, picking up his harmonica once again. "I'll be there."

Chapter
6

A few long days later, Hidalgo was galloping hard in a desolate area called the Empty Quarter when a bedu rider came out of nowhere. He was riding at full gallop when he passed Frank. Suddenly, a second rider appeared, passing at the same gait. A third rider went by, driving his horse even harder.

"They run pretty. But we last. Right, brother?" Frank reminded Hidalgo.

But Hidalgo was looking back over his withers, ears forward. His nostrils were twitching in the air and he was snorting agitatedly— something was not right.

Somewhere far out, a moaning sound seemed to come from the sand itself. The dunes appeared to be glowing and the horizon quickly melting. The sky had turned a striking yellow. A fourth rider appeared to come out of the strange light, whipping his horse. As he passed Frank, the rider looked over his shoulder with terror in his eyes.

"Easy," Frank said as Hidalgo tossed his head.

The horse backed up nervously. Frank stared intently, trying to understand what was happening. A strong wind came up. Frank's hat blew off but was held on by the stampede string around his neck. The earth seemed to come to life as more and more sand was lifted into the air in a spooky, swirling motion. It was a sandstorm!

The air howled. The tidal wave of sand began to mount and engulf the riders. Hidalgo ran like the wind—but the wind was winning.

Ahead, Frank spotted a crumbling ruin. It was an ancient fortress abandoned to the desert.

Frank and his horse, Hidalgo, have
never lost a long-distance race.

**Frank and Hidalgo find work with
Buffalo Bill's traveling Wild West Show.**

**Frank accepts a challenge to
race in an exotic far-off land.**

The American cowboy intrigues the sheikh.

The race begins as the horses
charge across the starting line!

The Ocean of Fire is a grueling race across 3,000 miles of desert.

The sheikh's evil nephew, Katib, and his raiders
attack the camp to steal the mighty horse al-Hattal.

Jazira's faithful bodyguard, Jaffa, fights
to the death to save her from Katib.

**Racing neck and neck with al-Hattal,
Hidalgo pours on a last burst of speed . . .**

. . . to reach the finish line first.

Frank and Hidalgo win the Ocean of Fire!

Frank uses his prize money to save
a herd of wild mustangs from death.

Frank watches Hidalgo join the herd.
They are both finally free.

The sand bit into Hidalgo's flanks. The cowboy did his best to ride Hidalgo toward the ruined barracks. Together they closed their eyes against the swirling sand. Frank held on tight, hoping to survive the deafening sounds as the sand cut into them like needles. Then in an instant, everything went white.

Later, Frank emerged from the ruin to witness a change in the mysterious desert. What once had been rocky ground was now a sea of low dunes stretching off to the horizon. Frank navigated Hidalgo across this new terrain. They rode until sunset.

At the halfway checkpoint, a smaller version of the tent city was laid out on the sands near a camel road. A gritty wind still gusted.

At the food tent, the rider crews gathered to feast. As they shoved and pushed for scraps of bread, a great trilling sounded. It was Bin al-Reeh! He trotted in, exhausted and sweat-soaked.

The sheikh emerged from his wind-rippled

tent and looked on with pride. Behind him stood the veiled Jazira. Lady Anne came out of her white tent to observe.

The sheikh approached his stallion and touched his muzzle with fatherly admiration. "You are carried by the west wind itself," he said.

"How many have fallen?" the prince inquired, clearly exhausted.

"More than sixty riders have fallen out. Another thirty are unaccounted for," reported the sheikh.

The prince was about to begin an early celebration when a shout was heard. All eyes looked to the dunes. A rider approached in silhouette. He was slow and staggering, but still he approached. It was Lady Anne's Kurdish champion!

"We have one full day's rest before the long march to Iraq," said Lady Anne to her exhausted rider. "Al-Hattal has proven he can do it inside of eight days. You must maintain the pace. Do you hear me? Look at me!"

The rider looked at Lady Anne and tried to focus. Clearly he was frightened of her, but he barely had his wits about him at the moment.

And then, like a mirage, another silhouette appeared over the dune.

"Apple of Sodom . . . ," whispered the sheikh.

Jazira could not believe it, either. She smiled behind her veil.

Frank appeared with his bandana up over his mouth and nose. The American myth and his horse were alive in the foreign desert.

Frank ignored the offer of water from the slaves but quickly led Hidalgo to a trough.

"You survived the Jinnis of the Waste," said Yusuf, icing Hidalgo's sore legs. "Allah must have a more severe judgment awaiting you."

"You're all encouragement, ain't you?" muttered Frank as he watched the prince eyeing him. "You better up your price at the next cantina, pal."

"You have not seen the desert until you

cross the sands of the Hammad. So do not smile yet, *farengi*," warned the prince. He was sure the cowboy would not survive all the hardships the desert had in store for the riders.

That night, Frank was busy examining Hidalgo's legs when he saw a small figure slipping into his tent. It took a longer look for Frank to realize that it was Jazira. She signaled for him to remain quiet. "Please . . . ," she whispered.

"Don't look at you, right?" Frank said.

"There is no need to, Mr. Frank. Only to listen. There will be no grazing for the next one hundred miles," she told him.

"I can pack some barley," Frank said. But Jazira opened a sack and spilled a pile of dates onto Frank's blanket. He looked at her, confused.

"Trust me," she said. "Take with you this skin. It is filled with the butter of camel. Mix it with water for both you and your horse. It will keep you alive across the Hammad."

Frank looked at her, even though she had

forbidden it. She quickly glanced away, only to look back.

"It's time to lay the cards on the table, lady. Why you trying to help me?" Frank asked.

"Prince Bin al-Reeh owns many villages and vast lands," Jazira explained. "If he wins the race on al-Hattal, he is not only wealthier, but he receives property from my father. I do not wish to become his fifth wife, the youngest of his harem. I do not know if you are as good as it is said. But I have faith in the painted stallion."

Frank thought for a moment. "What would your father do if he found you in here?"

"It is not proper for me to speak of such violence," she answered.

"Great," Frank said, shaking his head.

Outside his tent, Frank could see Jaffa's outline, pacing back and forth with his sword drawn.

"Al-Hattal is greatness on four legs," Jazira said. "I trained him from a colt—I know. The English lady's chestnut is most excellent. And

Sakr the Falcon Man rides the daughter of a great champion of Dubai. But it is your little horse that holds something in the eye that I have never seen. It is spoken that you captured him in the wild."

"Badlands," Frank answered. "Long time ago."

"How did you tame him?" Jazira asked.

"I didn't," said Frank.

Jazira was staring at his unshaven face in the glow of the lantern. When his eyes locked on hers, she quickly lifted her veil to cover more of her face.

"Why do you cover?" Frank asked.

"It is our law. I am not to unguard my modesty to any man but my father, my husband-to-be, or unmarrying men like Jaffa," she told.

"I see. . . ."

"Forgive me, but you do not see," said Jazira. "You do not know our world."

Jazira went to the tent door. As she checked to see if the coast was clear, she spotted Frank's spur. She touched it and gently rolled it between her fingers. Fascinated, she turned to prolong their conversation.

"My father speaks five languages. He reads many books from the outside world. But his true enjoyment of literature, it is of Wild Bill and Calamity Jane."

Frank laughed in disbelief. "You're boshin' me."

"Please," she said. "Tell me, in this Wild West, there are nomads also? The red people. Like the Bedawi, they are a horse culture. Have you seen their vanishing kind?"

Frank grew quiet. "I am their kind," he finally said. "My father was a cavalry scout in charge of transporting a band of Sioux to the agency. Fell in love with the chief's daughter. Married her. My father called me Frank T. My grandmother called me Blue Child."

"I would know you only as a white man," said Jazira.

"Maybe I've gotten good at hiding my face, too," Frank said.

"Why?" she inquired.

"You don't know our world," he said.

Jazira stared at Frank intensely. Suddenly, a shadow appeared outside the tent. It was a figure unsheathing a large sword right behind Jazira. Quickly, Frank shoved the princess to the ground and threw himself on top of her to shield her from harm. Aziz cut the tent flaps and glowered over them. Jaffa stood behind him. He had been unable to stop the nosy Aziz from intruding, and now he had to play along with the unfortunate scene taking place in front of him.

All they saw was an American cowboy and an Arab woman—the sheikh's daughter, no less! Jazira seemed to be struggling to get out from under Frank.

"Foolish is a foreigner," said Jaffa with threatening eyes.

Moments later in the great tent, the sheikh sat solemnly sipping strong coffee from a small, delicate cup not much bigger than a thimble. Opposite him sat his daughter, Jazira. Her veil was off, but she was unable to look her father in the eye.

"Allah has decided that I should not sleep well these nights," said the sheikh. "My daughter has brought disgrace on this house. I am sickened."

"It is not how it appears to be," she pleaded.

"The unbeliever forced you into his quarters," he said.

"No. I went there by my own volition," she said. "I wished only to speak with him. He did not touch your daughter but tried to protect her from what he thought was danger. I am responsible."

The sheikh sipped his coffee. "Have you ever considered poisoning me, Jazira? Why torture me with such slow precision?"

"Why do you force me to marry a man who has never once looked at me?" she said defiantly.

"If he looks at you, I'll have to cut off his head. You are not yet his property," said the sheikh matter-of-factly.

"The women of the northern tribe no longer wear the veil," said Jazira.

"Pray you were a daughter of the northern tribe. Then I would not be in this untenable position. And in the middle of the great race! Shame upon you," he scolded.

"Shame upon *you*, Father, for allowing me to ride horses when no one sees. For taking me on gazelle hunts when the men make pilgrimage."

"You are all I have," he said kindly. "You are my treasure."

"But when the eyes of the people are on the great sheikh, I am lowly." Jazira then saw the armed guards appear in the doorway with Aziz. They were holding Frank at gunpoint. "Let him go," she begged.

The sheikh began to tremble with rage. "How dare you give orders to a man! In my tent! Aziz, remove a certain woman to the tent of office."

"No! It is not right!" screamed Jazira. But it made no difference. She was forcibly removed, kicking and screaming.

A few moments later, Frank was shackled and chained to a brass pole. In the back of the tent stood Jaffa, Aziz, and the gloating prince. The sheikh stood in front of him. He spoke clearly.

"It is written, Mr. Hopkins: if any of our chaste women commits lewdness with evidence against her, so shall she be confined until death claims her. Those who committed the crime with her must be stoned. And it is by law that the father must then drown his own daughter."

"Wasn't her—" Frank tried to interrupt, but swords went up. He did not go on.

"However," continued the sheikh, "we are far from the next cistern, and water is precious. I could drown Jazira in gin, but Major Davenport would fall victim to a severe melancholy, and then who would play bridge with me? So my decision is swift: for her trespass, my daughter will be flogged. Seven stripes. At a time hence. And you, an impure believer in the presence of a man who can trace his very blood back to Adam . . . you will be removed of your infidel self."

"Removed of my what?" asked Frank.

"Like a stallion not worthy of breeding,"

said the sheikh. Then he called for the camel skinner.

Frank's cheeks went pale. A small man stepped forward and placed a box before him. Inside, blades of various sizes rested on a velvet lining. At the sheikh's gesture, everyone left the tent. Frank began to drip with sweat as the camel skinner produced a long Turkish blade and rubbed it with hot oil. The sheikh got up and took one last look at Frank.

"The law of the desert is an inviolable one, Mr. Hopkins. I feel compassion for you. But I will not let your fear move me. So speak honestly as a man: did you violate my daughter?"

"No, sir," said Frank immediately.

"Can one believe an unbeliever?" asked the sheikh.

"Only fools and gamblers walk behind a strange mare. You can believe that," Frank said defiantly.

The sheikh stopped in his tracks, perplexed. "Is this a passage from the Bible?"

"No," Frank said. "Just something that Wild Bill said to me one night."

The sheikh stared at the foreigner, deciphering what he had said. The camel skinner undid Frank's empty holster.

"Do you refer to the man known as Wild Bill Hickock? The master of the double six-gun?" asked the sheikh.

"Only one Wild Bill, sir," said Frank as the skinner began to yank at his jeans. Frank kicked him with his boot heel, knocking him back.

"Hold your work," ordered the sheikh as he began to follow a new line of thought.

Later, the sheikh sat across from Frank, holding the Colt pistol in his hands. He turned it over in the lantern light to admire the craftsmanship. "Hickock was the true prince of pistoleers, was he not?"

"Pretty good with a twist draw," said Frank, and he told the sheikh a few tales about his hero.

"What does my daughter say about your horse?" asked the sheikh.

"She is a lady with an eye for horseflesh, sir. Has a way with the ponies, I'd say."

The sheikh aimed the Colt at the tent wall, enjoying the feel of it. Then he sank back into his bad mood. "She is a female—who has entered the sleeping quarters of an infidel."

Frank had to think fast. He needed to get the sheikh's mind off his daughter—and the camel skinner. "Ever hear of the OK Corral?"

"You were not there?" asked the sheikh in disbelief.

Frank winked. He knew bin Riyadh would appreciate the reference to the famous shoot-out, which might have been settled peacefully if not for the stubbornness of the cowboys involved. The sheikh smiled, thinking of the impossible situation he found himself in with this likable cowboy who was so very far from home. Finally he came to a conclusion and said, "Your punishment will be carried out when the race is done. Now tell me of this Wyatt Earp. . . ."

Chapter
7

Bloodcurdling screams came from outside the sheikh's tent. Javelins flew and guns fired. There was mayhem in the camp and the volley of gunfire. Hidalgo reared and pulled against his rope when he heard the other horses whinnying.

Just then, the leader of this fight appeared on horseback. It was Katib—the sheik's nephew. He had tried countless times to get his uncle to share his great breed of stallion, but the sheikh would not trust his worthless nephew with his family's prized horses. So Katib took matters into his own hands.

"Al-Hattal!" screamed Katib to his men. "Secure him!"

Inside the tent, the sheikh was about to unlock Frank's shackles. But one of Katib's men flew into the tent, rifle in hand. The sheikh grabbed one of the glistening swords hanging on the wall of the tent. With a powerful swing that belied his age, the sheikh met his attacker head on! Frank, still shackled, followed the sound of the thud. He stared in horror at the severed head that lay not four inches from his foot.

In a fury, the sheikh left the tent. Outside, he slashed through the raiders—he was a skilled swordsman. He fought his way through the camp and headed toward the prince's tent. The prince was already mounted on al-Hattal, preparing to flee. The sheikh shouted an order in Arabic, and the prince whipped the famed black stallion. Horse and rider thundered across the night sands.

Just then, a raider came up behind the sheikh, intending to stab him in the back with a dagger. The old sheikh wheeled with his sword, sending the man to his death.

Katib was frantically searching for the prize horse.

"Al-Hattal is gone!" shouted one of his soldiers.

Katib thrust his sword into his own man's throat. His eyes were wild in the flashing glow of the night fire.

Meanwhile, Jazira burst into her father's tent. She grabbed the key to unlock Frank's shackles. Their eyes met for a brief instant. Suddenly, a massive raider with multiple scars running down his face grabbed Jazira. Behind her, Aziz burst into the tent and began rummaging through the sheikh's things. He yanked back blankets and dug through the collection of Western dime novels.

"Aziz!" shouted Frank. "Get me out! Let me fight!"

But Aziz had other plans. He held up a leather book. A horse embossed in gold glittered on the cover. He held it close to his chest for a gleeful second, then shoved it into his robe and made his escape from the tent.

Frank wrestled in his shackles as the raider threw Jazira to the floor. She turned to face him with her father's brass coffeepot in her hand. She threw the steaming brew in his face. He doubled over and cursed as she ran quickly to unshackle Frank. But the raider grabbed her again and threw her across the room, into the hands of another raider, who dragged her away into the night.

The massive raider now came at Frank and swung his sword at the cowboy's chest. Frank ducked quickly. The sword hammered against the main tent pole. With all his strength, Frank slammed the raider in the face with the iron shackles on his wrist, felling the man. Frank ran out of the tent and through the camp amid the swords and javelins, gunfire and bellowing camels. He ran straight into the frantic sheikh.

"Where is my daughter?"

Before Frank could answer, two raiders bore down on the sheikh—both ready to hurl javelins through him. Just in time, Frank whipped out his Colt and took care of the attackers. The sheikh stared in awe at the shackled man's skill. Then he spun around and sank his sword into a raider who had been about to kill Frank from behind.

Jaffa ran breathless to the sheikh with news. "Katib has taken her. You may strike out both my eyes."

Distraught, the sheikh looked out across the sand. Frank ran to the edge of the camp, searching the darkness for any sign of her. But there was nothing to see. Jazira was gone.

Chapter 8

When the dust settled and the camp was finally quiet, the prince returned with al-Hattal. The sheikh was inside his tent, feeling angry and confused.

"Most men would fall prostrate and pray with gratitude that their daughter was taken in place of their finest horse," the sheikh said.

"You care for her," Frank said, strapping on his holster. "What are these people going to do with her?"

The sheikh sighed. "If I turn over al-Hattal, Katib will return my child."

"And if you don't?" Frank asked.

"He is the unlawful son of a jackal. He will

have his Gypsies commit crimes upon her. He will most likely cut off her left hand and send it to me in an incense box to persuade me in my thinking." The sheikh paced around the tent, trying to gather his thoughts. He looked through his ransacked things to make sure everything was still there. He threw back a rug and swept his hand over the floor in a panic—something was missing! "The al-Khamsa manuscripts. My family's breeding book. Where is it?" He furiously looked around the tent for the book. It was one of his family's most prized possessions. The book contained the ancient secrets of horse breeding and the family bloodline of al-Hattal.

"Bring your deputy in here," suggested Frank.

That morning, Frank stood and watched a terrible ceremony. Aziz knelt on the ground, hands tied behind his back. The sheikh stood over him, his sword drawn. "I will ask you once more, Aziz, and only once. Where did they take my daughter?"

"I know nothing!" insisted Aziz. "I only took the book to protect it from the raiders. Alas, they stole it from me."

The sheikh had no more patience with his deputy. "Stole it? Or paid you, my trusted brother?"

"It matters only to him," said Aziz. "Please, strike off my head and end my humiliation."

The sheikh drew a breath and hefted his sword. He was about to bring it down when Frank stepped in and kicked Aziz square in the ribs.

"What are you doing?" shouted the sheikh. "I must cut off his head!"

Frank grabbed Aziz and yanked him to his feet. "That's the fast way out, Aziz. And you ain't getting it."

Frank punched Aziz in the jaw and watched him fall to the ground. As he lay in the sand, Frank pivoted on his heel and placed one of his sharp spurs against the traitor's throat. Aziz pleaded for Frank to stop.

Frank said, "That's called a Mexican tattoo, deputy, and it lasts much longer than a sword. In fact, it can go all night. You had your chance."

"No!" shouted Aziz. "I know where they have taken her. Until they receive the stallion."

The sheikh and Frank exchanged looks. Then the sheikh gestured for Frank to follow him a few yards away.

"I know you are not a gambling man," said the sheikh. "But bring Jazira back by nightfall . . . and you are forgiven."

"And the race?" Frank asked.

"Return her to my caravan by then and I will permit you to rejoin the race," said the sheikh.

Frank stared out across the sands.

"Attempt to deceive me and run . . . and you will not get beyond the port of Jordan with your head."

Chapter 9

The next day, Frank rode Hidalgo across the Arabian Desert, following Aziz, who rode a donkey. Jaffa trailed on a Berber horse, leading al-Hattal. When they spotted the village where Katib was hiding, Frank turned to Aziz. "Jazira rides out safe, or you're free lunch for the coyotes."

As they rode through a filthy marketplace, they found the mosque where Katib had taken the sheik's daughter. Aziz announced to the guards that the sheikh's attendants wanted words with Katib.

The sheikh's murderous nephew walked out into the courtyard. He was so surprised to see the great al-Hattal delivered that he dropped his napkin. "Al-Hattal. The great one . . . Bring him to my stable."

"Bring Jazira to us," instructed Jaffa.

"I take al-Hattal to my stable, and then you shall see the child," Katib said.

"No," said Jaffa flatly.

Katib stared at the huge slave. He didn't want to give in, but the sight of the great horse made him greedy. Katib quickly agreed to the conditions.

Frank, who was wearing a head cloth to cover his Western face, was busy examining his surroundings for a quick getaway.

"My niece, I am sad to see you leave. But your father wished you home," said Katib to Jazira. Then he gestured for Jaffa to bring the great horse forward. Jazira caught Frank's shifting eyes and felt uneasy. She knew something bad was about to happen.

"You are magnificent," said Katib upon being handed the beautiful horse. Jaffa, Frank, and Jazira had begun to head toward the archway when something strange happened. Katib felt a foreign substance on his fingers. He looked at them and saw black dye staining his hand. Stunned for a moment, he rubbed his fingers together and smelled the dye on his hands. He grabbed the silk blankets covering the horse and ripped them away. There he saw that the horse was actually white—only the legs, head, and neck were dyed black. This was not al-Hattal!

"*Kill her!*" shouted Katib.

Jaffa screamed and lunged toward the men who were chasing Jazira down. "Run!" he shouted, taking out his sword.

Frank and Jazira ran like the wind to get out, but one of Katib's guards got in the way. Frank took out his Colt and shot the man down. Just then, another man appeared and closed the heavy door they were hoping to use for escape. Katib, intent on killing Jazira himself, began firing. Frank shoved Jazira into a corridor and shot at Katib's gun, throwing off the other man's aim. Jaffa motioned for Frank to get Jazira out while he took care of the guards.

"Stop the foreigner!" shouted Katib.

Jazira was running like wildfire down the corridor of the mosque. When she found an altar at the end, she opened a trunk hidden beneath it and removed her father's manuscript from where Katib had hidden it. But four men were gaining on her. They were storming the alley with their swords drawn—Jazira had to get out!

And then he appeared! Charging toward her, Hidalgo whinnied and frothed as he searched for his master. The men closed in on Jazira as she ran alongside Hidalgo. She grabbed a handful of mane and mounted him at a run.

In the courtyard, Aziz aimed his rifle at the saddled Jazira. But just as he pulled the trigger, his rifle flew out of his hands with a clatter of steel. It was Jaffa—injured but still fighting, he had thrown his weapon at the gun. Katib's men rushed to impale Jaffa, now weaponless. With all the strength he had left, the giant managed to grab Aziz by the throat. As the hot taste of his own blood filled his mouth, Jaffa smiled proudly, knowing that he had bought Jazira a little time to escape—and that he was dragging the traitor Aziz into death's cold embrace along with him.

"Jaffa!" Jazira screamed. But there was nothing she could do. With an army of men chasing her, she reined Hidalgo hard and smashed into rows of cattle stalls, trying desperately to find daylight.

Meanwhile, Frank was running on top of the narrow wall that encircled the mosque. He could hear Hidalgo's galloping hooves, but he could not see him yet. And then he glimpsed her—Jazira skillfully riding his wild mustang, knocking over carts and barrels in the marketplace. One of Katib's men appeared in front of him, blocking his way. Frank turned to go in the other direction, but another armed man blocked him. They left him no choice. Frank jumped from the wall. He fell through the latticework of an arbor, landing square on Hidalgo's saddle behind Jazira. Together, they galloped away.

But it wasn't over. Katib was following them ferociously. Frank and Jazira had one more arch to clear, and then they would be home free.

But Katib was livid. He fired his rifle again and again. Jazira reined Hidalgo hard. With the sound of bullets cracking in the air, Hidalgo leaped over the last wall. They cleared it, Jazira holding on tightly to the reins and Frank poised with his Colt, watching their backs. The three of them had made it!

Katib came racing around the corner on his horse, barking more orders. He rallied his men. It would take more than an arm soaked in blood and a broken wrist to stop him from taking possession of al-Hattal.

Jazira prayed and wept in the open sands. Frank inspected Hidalgo to make sure he was not hurt.

"We need to reach the tent camp before sunup," he told her. He was worried that they would have unwanted visitors if they stayed too long.

"Please, I wish you to look at me," said Jazira. "Tell me why you did this. I find no reason in it."

Frank studied her eyes above the veil. She took his hand and lifted it to her chin, letting him know it was all right to unmask her. He studied her face in the light of the moon.

"Why do I feel that you truly see me . . . when others do not?" she whispered.

"Hidalgo trusts you," Frank said.

"And you?" she asked.

"Even a blind man could see that you are beautiful," Frank said. And with that he helped her onto Hidalgo. They were off again.

At high noon, Frank and Jazira made their way safely into the sheikh's camp.

"You are back in the great race, Frank Hopkins. If you so choose," said the sheikh. Frank had made him a very happy man. The cowboy was sitting by himself, drinking. He had been to war and back, and the ordeal was starting to take its toll. His only response to the sheikh was a small nod.

"Iraq will reduce that number to two," the sheikh continued, explaining the potentially fatal rigors that riders would face in the second half of

the race. "The Syrian desert . . . to one. Or none."
The sheikh started to walk away, then stopped in
his tracks. "Frank Hopkins, I am compelled to
express gratitude." The sheikh examined Frank's
face. As always, he was fascinated and disturbed
by the lonely emptiness he saw in the eyes of the
cowboy. The sheikh decided not to press the issue
of his gratitude. Thanks mattered little to the man
Frank Hopkins.

Chapter
10

Frank sat under the stars. Lady Anne approached him.

"You're a shrewd player, Hopkins," she said. "So I shall not condescend to you. There is no way for me to win the rights to the Muniqiyah bloodline other than by winning this race. You, on the other hand, have another way to win."

"Only one way to win," said Frank.

"Your little mustang has proven hardy. He's made it halfway. But your horse is weakening. And you know it. Are you willing to kill him for money?"

Lady Anne made Frank an offer. If he pulled out of the race now, she would give him a third of the winner's purse in silver.

"When you're racing in the desert," Frank said coolly, "green grass and water can be mighty tempting . . . but it just might be a mirage, too."

"What of my offer?" she asked him.

"I'll sleep on it," Frank said. He tipped his hat and walked away.

Poor Hidalgo was tired. Frank worried that another four hundred miles would put him lame. But Jazira had told Frank that he must not quit. He and Hidalgo had come too far.

The next morning, Frank crawled out of his tent. He looked around to greet Hidalgo—but his horse was gone! Frantic, he ran through camp until he saw something he could not believe. The prince was on al-Hattal at the starting line, the Kurdish champ waited on Lady Anne's chestnut, and even Sakr the Falcon Man sat atop his white bedu horse. And there stood Hidalgo at his mark, alone. He was waiting to race.

Frank picked up his things and walked to the starting line. It was time to go.

As Frank and Hidalgo moved across the black sands, the ground began to change. What once had been sand turned to sharp volcanic rock, blackened by the sun. It went on as far as the eye could see.

"We can do it," Frank said to Hidalgo. Hidalgo snorted. It was agreed. They *would* do it.

Meanwhile, Lady Anne and her caravan trotted along. A low rumble was heard in the distance. It was Katib and his men. They caught up to the caravan.

"You call yourself a great raider? For not being able to hold on to a little harem girl?" Lady Anne snapped.

"You will still pay me. Or I will exact it from you," said Katib.

"You'll receive nothing unless my Kurd reaches the finishing stone first," said Lady Anne. "They are six days across the Hammad. You can intercept them by the camel road. Force the American and the Falcon Man into the Umm al-Samim. Capture al-Hattal and keep him secure. But my mare wins the race."

Katib gathered his men to go.

"He made you look the fool, didn't he? The cowboy humiliated you on your own lands," mocked the lady.

"I will find the *farengi*, Lady English. And he will beg me. He will beg me to cut his throat when I am done with him," swore Katib.

"Do not harm him," said Lady Anne. "Kill his horse. Make him walk the desert. There is much for him to think over."

Lady Anne watched as Katib took off. The race was beginning to wear on her soul.

Chapter
11

At sunrise, Frank awoke to the tickle of an insect crawling on his arm. It was a locust. He looked at Hidalgo and saw a locust crawling on his leg. Frank swept it off. And then a hum surrounded him. An ominous, far-off sound. Suddenly, he saw it coming toward them—like a tidal wave.

"Down!" Frank yelled.

They hit—hundreds of thousands of locusts buzzed in, pelting them like rocks. Frank quickly covered Hidalgo with his bedroll. They remained as still as they could until the insect storm passed. And as quickly as they had come, the menacing insects were gone. The quiet whisper of the desert wind returned, and Frank looked around at dead locusts strewn over the sand, left in the wake of the swarm.

Then Frank remembered Jazira's words. "The locusts are a gift from above. Not a plague, as we believe." He squatted and picked up a carcass. Slowly, he brought the bug to his mouth. He hesitated, then popped it into his mouth. Frank crunched down on the insect. Hidalgo snorted and backed away.

"Get past the legs and they ain't so bad," Frank said, offering one to Hidalgo. "If they can survive, we can survive."

Day turned into night and back into day as Frank rode Hidalgo through the endless desert. The heat was nearly unbearable, not to mention their thirst and exhaustion. Frank made sure to check his horse's pulse often, always worrying that he was working Hidalgo too hard. And Frank had to tie himself to his mount so as not to fall off.

Far out in the desert, Sakr the Falcon Man rode alone. He whipped his white horse and pushed hard—and then the earth suddenly opened up beneath him! Sakr had hit the Umm al-Samim, the Arabian Desert's scorching quicksand.

Sakr's white mare panicked. She pawed into the quicksand, reared, and threw Sakr straight off her back. The horse was nimble and fast enough to get her legs out of the melting sand, but not Sakr. The melting desert sand was swallowing the falconer.

Sakr's horse tried to help him, but when her leg was nearly sucked in again, she fled in fear, leaving her master to drown in the sand.

Lady Anne's Kurdish champion led his horse around the quicksand. He passed Sakr, who was sinking into the ground and screaming from the heat of the sand. The Kurd plodded ahead, never looking back.

Frank found Sakr still struggling in the sand. He tried to help, but Sakr wouldn't have it. He asked Frank to throw him his scimitar and leave him to his fate. Frank obliged. He had long since accepted that the rules of the West didn't apply in this faraway desert.

The next day in the dunes of Syria, the prince was still in the lead. He rode on proudly, confident of his position in the race. But the prince heard a far-off sound and turned around to look. He could not believe his eyes. In the distance, coming toward him, was the American!

Then Lady Anne's chestnut appeared. Frank and the Kurdish champion were riding neck and neck for second place.

The prince, with panic in his eyes, dug his heels into his horse and picked up his gait. But soon enough, all three horses and their riders were in a cluster—the prince, the Kurdish champ, and the cowboy. All keeping the same pace.

Seemingly out of nowhere, five of Katib's thugs appeared, trying to circle the riders. The prince sped up and managed to get away. The Kurd did the same. Now the five men were surrounding Frank and Hidalgo. Frank managed to break free and Hidalgo took off, but not for long. Hidalgo and Frank fell into a ten-foot pit—it was a trap in the sand! Hidalgo whinnied in panic. Frank held on to the javelin that had been set in the pit to impale him. Frank checked Hidalgo. A second javelin had pierced the horse's flesh. Blood soaked Frank's hands.

"*No!*" cried Frank.

"*Farengi!*" said a voice from above the pit. "Do you not know how we catch gazelles in the Syrian desert?" It was Katib, and he was aiming his rifle straight into the pit. "The great law compels me to allow you to shoot your own animal in compassion."

Frank reached for his Colt, but it was missing, lost in the tumble. Just then, a brigand joined Katib at the edge of the pit and aimed his rifle at Frank.

"You heard the Christian woman," Katib said in Arabic. "We are not to kill him. The desert will know that honor." Katib pushed the barrel of the gun away from the pit. He looked down one last time. Then Katib mounted his horse and ordered his caravan to find the prince next.

Down in the pit, Frank threw his shoulder into Hidalgo, desperately trying to shift the horse's eight hundred pounds from the javelin. But he couldn't. Frank pulled out his knife and quickly cut into the flesh around Hidalgo's wound. Hidalgo brayed in pain, thrashing wildly. As awful as it was, it had to be done, and it freed Hidalgo from the shaft of the javelin.

Then a shadow was cast into the pit. Frank looked up to see the face of Sakr, the falconer.

"The rope! Quickly!" Sakr shouted. Frank didn't have time for reasoning, so he looped his rope around Hidalgo's neck. Then he hurled the other end up to Sakr.

"Hurry!" Sakr yelled, tying the rope to his Arabian. The white horse began to pull, trying to free Hidalgo from his trap.

In the distance, Katib and his men spotted Sakr at the lip of the pit. Cursing and screaming, Katib ordered his men to open the horse-drawn covered box behind them. In a flash, two leopards were let loose. They raced toward the pit!

Hidalgo was pawing the sand and kicking with his powerful rear legs. Frank rammed the javelins into the sand wall to act as stairs. The mustang fought his way up until he finally exploded onto the sand, breathing hard and bleeding heavily.

Flying over the sand like a spotted bullet, one of the leopards hurled itself through the air and landed on the white mare. The mare whinnied as she tumbled to the ground, throwing Sakr into the air. The mare escaped the leopard and took off into the desert. The angry leopard sped off in hot pursuit.

Instantly, the second cat appeared and bore down on Hidalgo. The horse reared up and brought his front hooves crashing down on the trained cat.

One of Katib's men attacked Sakr, but Frank hurled one of the javelins at the man. It soared through the air and impaled the attacker.

Meanwhile, Hidalgo continued to fight the savage leopard. As the cat recoiled for another attack, Hidalgo struck a brutal blow with his hooves, crushing the leopard's skull.

Another of Katib's mercenaries galloped in with a ready rifle, but Sakr's falcon flew into his head with its own skull-crushing force. Immediately, the bird began to claw at the man's eyes. The man screamed and fell from his horse.

Katib rode in, brandishing a British pistol. Sakr ran toward the vile man with his sword poised to strike. Katib fired three times, shooting the falconer dead.

Katib then noticed the unarmed Frank and smiled. The sheikh's nephew dismounted his horse, holstering his pistol and drawing his bloodstained sword. Frank frantically looked for a weapon, but all he had handy was a javelin. It was no match for the glistening sword.

"You and your horse have made trouble for me, cowboy. You both will die now." Katib charged Frank with his sword. Frank thrust his javelin, but it broke on Katib's sword.

Katib pressed forward, swinging for Frank's head. He prepared to finally impale Frank.

Frank fell to the ground, raising his broken javelin to ward off the blow. He kicked upward and connected with Katib's stomach, sending him into the air. Katib landed hard on his back and scrambled to get to his feet. But the ground around him was trembling—something was wrong. Sand began to sift around him through a thousand tiny slots. Katib realized he was standing on the roof of another gazelle trap!

Now it was Katib's turn to sweat. If he were to move an inch, the earth would give. So he stood there, motionless.

Picking up his Colt from the sand, Frank whistled for Hidalgo. He pulled a lariat from his saddle. Katib smiled, thinking the cowboy intended to help him. But Frank had other plans.

"No one hurts my horse and lives," said Frank, skillfully roping the stick that would trigger the trap. He gave the rope a hard, grim pull. The ground gave way, and Katib fell to a gruesome death on the spikes below.

Chapter 12

Hours later, Frank shuffled through the sand. Hidalgo nudged his cowboy, but Frank was too tired to feel it. Hidalgo tried to do it again, but his legs buckled beneath him. Finally, the weary horse collapsed, crashing onto the sand. Frank knelt down, trying to keep Hidalgo's head from hitting the scorching sand. Blood was frothing at the horse's muzzle.

"It's all right. Easy," soothed Frank, trying to easy the horse's pain. "Don't you do it now, partner. Don't you die on me now. We're almost home."

Hidalgo did not respond. He lay on his side, one eye to the sun. Frank lowered the mustang's head onto the sand, and then he got up with a struggle. He began to tell Hidalgo old tales of races they had won together. At the same time, Frank was dusting off his old Colt. He put a bullet in the chamber. Frank looked up and scanned the great expanse of desert he'd have to walk alone, and then he put in one more bullet.

Hidalgo looked at Frank for comfort.

"It's all right, brother," Frank lied. He pointed the gun at his horse, hands trembling. But a noise came from the horizon. Frank looked and saw nothing. He turned back again to pull the trigger, but he heard the far-off noise again.

Frank began to see Lakota Ghost Dancers in the distance—but it was a mirage. Being out in the desert heat for that long without much food or water would disorient even the best of men. Frank stumbled to his knees and started singing the Lakota death song.

When he heard Frank singing, Hidalgo tried to lift his head, but it was no use.

A bird circled overhead. An eagle, thought Frank. But he was too delirious to realize it was a falcon. Sakr's falcon! The bird circled, screeched twice, and dropped something onto the sand. Frank crawled over to it. It was a clamshell, maybe an oyster. But what was a shell doing out in the desert? Frank picked it up and stared off into the distance. A huge shadow fell over him. It was Hidalgo—a bit unsteady but standing!

"I smell it, too. The ocean," said Frank weakly. "The ocean."

Hidalgo took a step forward. Frank grabbed his stirrups and pulled himself to his feet. He removed the heavy saddle from Hidalgo and left it lying in the desert. Frank mounted the horse bareback. They were off again!

Hidalgo tried to keep on his feet with everything he had left. Frank was in a complete daze. Together they carried on. When Hidalgo whinnied, Frank looked up to see Lady Anne's chestnut ahead. And no more than fifty yards ahead of that was the prince.

"All we have to do is last," said Frank, patting Hidalgo's head.

The prince smelled the sea and knew it was

time. He stopped to get a final drink from his water bag. He looked behind; the Kurd was coming up on his left, and the cowboy on his right.

"Cowboy, you will not defeat me!" shouted the prince when Frank was in earshot. "I am born of a great tribe, people of the horse. I am of the blood of warriors!"

"So am I!" said Frank proudly as he rode defiantly onward.

This was it! The last five miles of torture. The prince and the Kurd were a mile apart. But the prince was slightly ahead. The Kurd yanked his reins and took off.

The prince felt the charge from behind him. He lifted his tasseled crop high and brought it down on al-Hattal's flank. The stallion arched his neck and lurched forward.

In the distance, the cheering could be heard. The finish line was surrounded by onlookers. And their shouts encouraged the prince. Al-Hattal was on fire to be the first across the line! They were in the lead.

Meanwhile, the lady's chestnut mare was neck and neck with Hidalgo. The mare swung her head and tried to take a bite out of Hidalgo. The mustang leapt aside of the mare's gnashing teeth. He poured on a bit more speed.

"Not yet. Hold!" instructed Frank.

The mare and the mustang's hooves pounded the sand, each animal driving the other with their fury to win. Frank threw his cowboy hat to the sand and howled, "Let 'er buck!" And with that, Hidalgo ignited. He galloped ahead of the mare. The Kurd screamed, trying to spook Hidalgo. But nothing could stop Hidalgo now.

Frank was now in second place.

The prince caught sight of the finishing stone. His teeth clenched and his head cloth trailed like a wild kite.

But Frank and his horse were not too far behind. They were raring. They hadn't come this far to finish second.

As they gained on the prince, the Kurd made a comeback! He rode even harder, sliding the sharp steel of his dagger into the skin of his mare. She rocketed forward.

The crowd at the finish line went into a frenzy.

Out of the corner of his eye, the prince saw a rider. When he realized it was the cowboy, he screamed a war cry and summoned all he had left to win. But Frank had a cry of his own—a Lakota war cry that sent a shiver down the spines of everyone at the finish line.

It was the last hundred yards. For Frank, all sounds went quiet but one: the beating heart of Hidalgo!

In the distance, six judges watched as the three horses bore down on the finish line.

Hidalgo's eyes were wild and his wounds were burning, but he raced.

The three riders were neck and neck. And then . . . Hidalgo broke away! He pulled ahead by twenty . . . thirty . . . forty yards! Hidalgo was gone!

Galloping hard, Hidalgo thundered across the finish line!

The onlookers of the tent city went wild.

Frank hugged Hidalgo's neck with pure joy and love.

Jazira looked stunned.

The sheikh was silent. He had to turn his head away for fear everyone would see the smile of admiration curling the corners of his mouth.

Lady Anne stared ahead, trying to accept her loss.

Hidalgo kept running, straight into the cool water of the sea.

Part of the crowd rushed after him to touch his flanks or pat Frank's back.

The Lakota flag was raised and waved over the crowd. It was glorious.

In the middle of all the celebration, the prince also rode down to the sea.

"He is a magnificent horse," the prince said to Frank.

"Likewise, prince," said Frank. The two tired men gave each other a nod of respect.

The prince turned his horse and led him to the water cisterns, where he could finally get a drink. The race was over. The prince had lost.

Frank dismounted and gave Hidalgo's neck another hug. "You did it, mustang. You're the king."

Chapter
13

Under the great tent, the sheikh and Frank sat drinking coffee.

"For many miles I did not understand why Allah would wish this on me. But now I understand His will. Desert law compels me to surrender the title of champion and bless you. And beseech you to be a guest in my house for as long as you desire."

"I've been too far from home for too long, sir," said Frank. And then, as if considering the kindness of the man's offer, he unholstered his beautiful Colt and presented it to the sheikh.

"But I lost the race, Frank Hopkins," he said.

"But you won a friend," Frank said warmly. "It's a gift."

Outside the tent rows, Jazira was dressing Hidalgo's wounds.

"He'll miss you," said Frank from behind her.

"Is it true, then?" she asked, looking at Frank. "The cowboy rides away? Into the setting of the sun?"

"But not the same cowboy," said Frank.

Jazira smiled. "You and Hidalgo have won more than silver. You have shown many that it is not about blood and pedigree. It is much greater than that."

"I'll never forget you," said Frank. He tipped his hat to the beautiful woman whose world he did not, and would not ever, know. Then he walked off to be alone under the bright desert stars.

"Goodbye, Blue Child," Jazira whispered.

Chapter 14

Weeks later, at the Pine Ridge Indian Agency in South Dakota, a wagon stood stacked with government-issued rifles. A cavalry officer and two cattlemen were overseeing an operation, staring across the wagon at the fifteen men assembled there.

"Rifle and a box of cartridges to each man," instructed an officer to the motley band of hired mustang hunters.

"Yes, sir," they replied.

"Assemble on the rim, thirty paces to a stand," ordered the officer.

One of the cattlemen distributed the rifles. In a deep arroyo nearby stood thousands of starving wild horses, crowded together. On the dirt reservation road that passed the mustang corral, wagonloads of Lakota men and women stared sadly at the mustang death row. An old Lakota man sat beside the wagon driver with a sick, sorrowful look in his eyes.

"Move along now!" shouted the officer. "Let's go!"

But across the grassy bluffs, a horseman could be seen approaching.

"What's this buck doing? Bringing them in one at a time?" asked the officer.

Frank Hopkins rode in on Hidalgo. They both looked rested and refreshed. "Officer McNulty?"

"Who are you?"

"Name is Hopkins. Frank Hopkins."

"You bring a dispatch?" McNulty asked.

Frank nodded. He opened his saddlebag and removed an official letter. "Read it."

As the officer read, a Lakota horse driver approached Frank. "You are the one they call Far Rider?"

"Is it true that the chief named Eagle Horn has returned to the agency?" Frank asked hopefully.

The driver nodded slowly.

"Can you take me to him?" Frank asked.

"He has taken the journey. But he knew Far Rider won. In the faraway sand."

Frank bowed his head in respect and sadness.

Frank and the Lakota driver stood at the gate that held the thousands of wild mustangs.

"Ready?" Frank asked.

As the Lakota man nodded, Frank pulled the wooden pin that held the gate closed. He pushed the gate, causing it to swing wide open, and scrambled out of the way as the wild horses thundered past. Out across the Great Plains ran the mustangs—freed from a death sentence. None of the men could hold back their smiles.

Frank had to grab Hidalgo's reins—the scent of freedom excited the mustang. Hidalgo drank the air and snorted it out. He breathed hard as he watched the stampede of mustangs.

Slowly, Frank removed the saddle blanket from Hidalgo's back. He moved close and looked Hidalgo in the eye. Frank grabbed the bridle and slipped it over Hidalgo's ears. Hidalgo shook his mane and ran forward, as if an electric current was coursing through him. But he circled back and returned to Frank. Frank looked him in the eye again, causing Hidalgo to snort. But the horse kept one eye on the wild horses running free.

"Run, Hidalgo. Go!"

Frank flapped his hat at Hidalgo, and he ran like the world champion he was. He whinnied at the wild horses ahead. But a hundred yards out, he stopped and turned. Standing in a regal posture, he looked at Frank for the last time.

"Let 'er buck!" Frank cried one last time.

And with that, Hidalgo reared. He turned and galloped away. He was wild and free.

Frank stood at the edge of the red mesa while a strong wind ripped at his coat. He looked over the Great Plains, seeing the wild horses in the distance. He wondered if it would be there forever, the real West—not Buffalo Bill's idea of it. The free West.

Then he turned and walked to where green grass met a blue sky that seemed to go on forever. Hidalgo was free now. So was Frank Hopkins.